The Mountain Grizzly

by
Michael S. Quinton

hancock

house

ISBN 0-88839-417-9
Copyright © 1999 Michael S. Quinton

Cataloging in Publication Data
Quinton, Michael S.
    The mountain grizzly

    ISBN 0-88839-417-9

    1. Grizzly bear--Rocky Mountains. 2. Grizzly bear--Rocky
Mountains--Pictorial works. I. Title.
QL737.C27Q56 1999   599.7'84   C97-910887-X

Editor: Nancy Miller
Production: Nancy Miller and Ingrid Luters
Cover Design: Ingrid Luters

Published simultaneously in Canada and the United States by

HANCOCK HOUSE PUBLISHERS LTD.
19313 Zero Avenue, Surrey, B.C. V4P 1M7
(604) 538-1114 Fax (604) 538-2262

HANCOCK HOUSE PUBLISHERS
1431 Harrison Avenue, Blaine, WA 98230
(604) 538-1114 Fax (604) 538-2262
Web Site: www.hancockhouse.com *email:* sales@hancockhouse.com

Acknowledgments

To my mom and dad, Ray and Bernadene Quinton, thank you for giving me the love of nature and opportunity to pursue my childhood dream of being a wildlife photographer. To my wife, Cindy, and our cubs, Rebecca and Joshua, thank you for your love and for putting up with this nature nut—I love you. To my friends Ron Shade, Brandon Wynn, Jeff Brough and Tim Bloxham, memories of your good-natured companionship will always be an inseparable part of the thrill, adventure, beauty, sweat and danger of stalking grizzlies in the wild. First-hand observations by Bruce Penske and Collin Gillan helped to pinpoint my photographic efforts. Thank you.

Meet the Mountain Grizzly

Early July found us high above timberline in western Wyoming on an extended assignment for a major magazine to photograph grizzly bears. Brandon Wynn, my two-legged pack animal, and I had come to this rugged wilderness to photograph a little-known behavior of a unique concentration of grizzly bears. The highest peaks drew grizzlies from afar to feed on aggregations of army cutworm moths. That's right, moths. The grizzlies fed almost exclusively on the moths which had migrated here from hundreds of miles away. The army cutworm moths would spend the hot months of July and August aestivating (essentially a summer hibernation) in the scree slopes one thousand feet above timberline.

Upon spotting six grizzlies on a single slope we began a long stalk. A sow and two very large cubs, perhaps two-and-a-half year olds, were busy moving the mountain. They stood on all fours with hind legs spread wide, and with their front paws sent an avalanche of rocks and boulders bouncing down the steep slope. Uncovering moths, they would poke their heads into a hole and lap up the insects, and then move to another spot and start over. They located the moths with their noses and ears. The moths sometimes fanned their wings deep in the scree and could be heard from above.

The grizzlies paid no heed to where they sent the boulders and it was each bear's responsibility to watch his own hide. On one occasion, the sow dislodged a huge boulder weighing tons and it headed straight toward one of the cubs. Seeing the boulder bearing down on him, the cub let out a roar and ran for his life. He moved uphill from his mom so he could forage safely. We could easily hear the commotion from over a mile away, the sound bouncing off sheer rock faces above the bears. Just then a large, dark sow with a pair of small cubs of that year appeared, the older family group quickly moved uphill avoiding the newcomers.

As a wildlife photographer, I have been privileged to have spent more than my share of time observing wildlife of North America's wilderness. I feel great satisfaction when I am able to capture on film a moment in the lives of any of the species which live in our wild mountains. Being an eyewitness to wildlife spectacles is my motive—I am a naturalist first, a photographer second. My fondest memories are days spent perched on a mountain ridge watching wild grizzlies.

All grizzlies, from the giant coastal brown bears of Alaska to the bears of Yellowstone's dry sagebrush meadows are the same species, *Ursus arctos*. This book focuses on the interior grizzlies of the mountainous regions of the U.S. and Canada along the Continental Divide in the Rocky Mountains north through British Columbia, Yukon and Alaska's vast interior. These interior or mountain grizzlies are generally smaller than their coastal cousins because of severe mountain climates. However, not all mountain grizzlies are small. Boars more than 1,000 pounds have been weighed in Yellowstone, but more commonly adults reach only 300 to 500 pounds. Grizzlies may live more than twenty years in the wild.

I have met the mountain grizzly on his turf among the wild mountains from Wyoming to Alaska, I have found no differences in the bears of distant regions, save their feeding habits. As a photographic subject, grizzlies are difficult at best and generally stay out of camera range even with the most powerful telephoto lenses. The need and desire to photograph grizzlies always causes a certain amount of anxiousness—a mix of dread and excitement. I would prefer to just watch the great bears from a distance and let them go about their business undisturbed. On occasion, however, I have been lucky and persistent enough to have been within camera range to preserve moments of their secretive lives.

Just getting into camera range of the ever-alert, moth-eating grizzlies was a hit-and-miss proposition. We turned our attention to the newcomers, the big sow and small cubs who moved onto the scree slope and displaced the other sow and her two-and-a-half year olds. Brandon and I began closing in on the bears as they mothed. This sow, too, paid no attention to where she heaved the boulders and the cubs stayed out of the way. The cubs were busy sticking their snouts into the cracks in the rocks, but they could not move the big boulders and get at the moths.

We entered a boulder field below the feeding grizzlies where the overhead cliff had collapsed many years before, leaving a jumble of cabin-sized boulders. The danger of a sudden, close-range encounter with an unseen bear was very real. I led the way slowly with my tripod and telephoto over my shoulder and bear spray, with the safety off, in the other hand ready for close combat. As we moved into camera range, cover grew scarce and we cautiously moved from one small boulder to another to stay out of sight.

Suddenly a nerve-wracking roar and bawling erupted and echoed off the cliff walls of the mountain cirque. One of the cubs was bawling in pain. We were horrified to see the sow was mauling its own cub. The severe punishment came when the cub stuck his nose into mom's moth hole—apparently a terrible sin. The cub lay a fury heap among the rocks without movement. The sow continued her mothing. We feared she had injured the cub, even killed it. I was snapping a couple pictures when a light breeze moving uphill carried our scent to the sow. She snorted and raised up high on hind legs and waved her big snout back and forth smelling. Dropping down to all fours, she coughed a warning and began a hasty retreat across the boulders and away from us.

The cub, who had not so much as twitched an ear, suddenly sprang to life and followed its mother, bouncing from rock to rock to rock. The family of grizzlies moved across the mile-wide basin of scree and snowfields, stopping a couple of times to look in our direction. They then climbed up a 12,000-foot ridge along steep snowdrifts. Nearing the top they jumped a small red fox who streaked away and then sat down to watch the bears. The bears, too, stopped to look at the fox. One of the cubs then slowly approached the sow with obvious caution. It was received with a loving face licking. The cub had been forgiven. The family then carried on and disappeared over the crest.

Of the thirteen grizzlies we observed mothing in this locale, she was the dominant bear. Every bear they encountered gave her a wide berth. She had power and her will was law in these parts. She had no need for tolerance. Brandon and I were the only subjects in her kingdom who hadn't yet gained respect for her power, courage and aggression.

We moved our spike camp a few miles into another high basin where a sow and her three cubs of the year were mothing. We pitched camp at timberline in a stand of subalpine fir and whitebark pine a mile from the scree slopes. Brandon climbed a tall, lightning-killed fir to attach a pulley for hanging our food, and then started to glass for bears. Almost immediately I spotted the sow and her three cubs running up a long, narrow snowdrift. They were spooked. We feared that they had winded us already. Then I saw what they were running from. A couple hundred yards below the sow and cubs loped a large male following their trail.

The sow led her cubs uphill through the steep talus to the base of a huge cliff. There she took refuge behind a large boulder. The boar soon turned back. I guess sore feet and facing a mad mother grizzly were not worth the chance of making a meal out of a cub. The sow nursed her cubs behind the boulder. Brandon and I worked our way up the rocky slope to await the return of the sow and her cubs. While waiting, I picked up the small, crushed skull of a grizzly cub. Had this cub been killed by an aggressive boar the year before? Perhaps this same male?

Finally the sow led her cubs back down from the cliff to a snowdrift. The cubs ran ahead, reaching the drift before their mother and began sliding down with apparent joy and careless abandon. The danger from the male now forgotten, it was time for a good roll in the snow. Far below we could see the adult male who had dropped down below the scree and was himself having a good time turning somersaults in the soft tundra.

The sow moved straight to where she could dig for moths about 400 yards from where Brandon and I watched. We stalked her. As we moved into camera range, about 150 yards away from the sow, I stepped onto a large, flat rock that tipped with a clunk. The sow snapped to attention. She stared in our direction, coughed and began moving out with her three cubs in tow. I'm sure she thought the boar was again after her cubs and this time she cleared out leaving this basin. There we were again, bear photographers without any bears.

A month later we were back in this western Wyoming wilderness of high alpine basins and peaks. We had just returned from an equally rugged and beautiful mountain setting in Montana where another grizzly population also spent the summer feeding on the army cutworm moths.

We saw the same bears that we had photographed a month earlier and how they had grown. We could hardly recognize them. They all had brand new fur coats that rippled when they walked and glistened in the sun. We made a successful stalk arriving at a point about 120 yards from the bears. For an hour I was able to photograph the moth eaters by snapping the shutter when the wind would cover the sound or when the sow had her head deep in a hole. Mostly I got pictures of bear rear ends poking skyward like big, furry boulders. All the action was down in the rocks. Even so, I was getting rarely photographed behavior. Unfortunately, when one is in camera range of a grizzly, one is also within the grizzly's hearing range. I snapped a photo when the wind had calmed down, and she heard me. She gathered up her cubs and headed out across the rocks. They moved about a mile and were about to disappear over a ridge when she suddenly changed course and dropped back down the slope toward us. She traveled a couple hundred yards and, one at a time, all four bears just disappeared as if swallowed up by the earth. Through a spotting scope we could barely make out the dark entrance of a cave. The cave was at more than 11,000 feet elevation, and although we watched for hours they never came out. I ruled out approaching the hole, but it was tempting.

In another remote basin we found the big, dark, dominant sow and her two cubs. They also had new coats and fat bellies. We had been led to their location by a flock of more than 100 ravens who flew past several basins then entered this one and did not come out. Many times we had seen mothing bears surrounded by ravens who were mopping up those moths disturbed by the digging. The ravens would always fly away at first sight of us, but this sudden flight of ravens never seemed to alert the bear.

The following day we hiked into this new basin. It was several miles from our spike camp and we arrived late. It was midmorning when I spotted the big bear and her cubs in the rocks. She looked huge. We stalked the bears for pictures. We were almost in camera range when the sow suddenly stopped feeding and began to move off the scree under the cliffs directly toward us. No doubt she was done feeding for the morning and was headed down to spend the day loafing under the shade of whitebark pines at timberline below us. We quickly climbed a large boulder and I set up the camera. Brandon was gripping two cans of bear spray—safeties turned off. We were both unnerved by the sow's approach. On they came. At sixty yards I snapped a couple pictures. The click of the camera's shutter was picked up by the female grizzly and she stood up. She towered over a boulder as she looked and smelled. She was a huge bear and had a look which would send any bear in the country on a run for its life—a race between its front legs and hind legs, each set trying to be the first to put a mountain between them and the great she-bear.

We had no such choice. The sow dropped down behind the boulder. We expected the sow to be on the run when she came out from behind the boulder, but nothing happened. We waited, gripping our bear sprays. Then the bear moved out slowly, deliberately from behind the boulder her cubs, clearly nervous, tight against her bulk. She stopped and faced us. One cub stood placing a paw on the sow's rump for balance. The sow made a quick step toward us, ready to charge, then stopped to reconsider. She did not know what we were. She snarled showing us a fang then turned and walked away, never breaking into a run. Her priority was the safety of her cubs. She feared nothing save the unknown consequences of an encounter with her only enemy—man.

These encounters were serious and dangerous. Even so, we went unarmed, prepared for the risks as best we could. Many years before these encounters with the mountain grizzlies in Wyoming I had cast aside common sense and strayed across that blurred line, that safety net called distance, a breach of grizzly proto-col. It has been twenty years since I risked it all for the increased detail and drama that close range brings to a photograph.

The fury of a female protecting her cubs can be impressive beyond belief but it was always encounters with the solitary males that were the most dangerous. Perhaps the boars were less inclined to back down than a sow concerned with her cubs' safety. While in Alaska in the late 1970s I learned something about how close is too close.

I had gone to Denali National Park to photograph the wildlife of the northern wilderness and was very anxious to capture some of the mountain grizzlies on film. I had read all the literature about grizzlies and went north, determined to have some encounters of my very own. My early attempts to photograph grizzlies were frustrating. The bears were hard to find and after a long stalk they avoided me by running away. Not the least of my bear photography problems was my inadequate lenses. Though I was armed with a brand new Nikon F with motor drive and a 500-mm lens, I was undergunned. I had to be within fifty yards of an adult grizzly to get full-frame photos. The blond grizzlies of the tundra were easy enough to spot, but there was no cover for stalking and no trees to climb, leaving this grizzly bear photographer want-to-be with a bad case of that age-old phobia of finding one's self at school clad only in underwear—in other words—exposed to the elements. After one long stalk over the open tundra I managed to get myself in position ahead of a sow and two cubs grazing my way. The sow noticed me when she was still 200 yards away and quickly moved her cubs away. So much for the idea that grizzlies possess poor eyesight. The bears moved to a grassy gully in full bloom with wildflowers when a big boar appeared grazing toward them. The boar swung his massive head back and forth biting and pulling up mouthfuls of grass. The sow quickly led her cubs away once again. I moved toward the boar but it snapped its head up and stared at me for a few seconds then proceeded to graze. I began taking pictures of the boar even though he was a bit out of range. But at least I was a bear photographer now. I was content to keep my distance, this time.

Several days later I again spotted this boar fast asleep in broad daylight. I slowly stalked the boar and sat down 100 yards away and waited for him to wake up. Every few minutes the boar would raise his big head, take a look around and smell the air. Several times he looked right at me but then dropped his head and went back to sleep. He knew I was there but chose to ignore me, I was elated. After his nap, the sun-bleached bear, rose and began to graze along a small creekbank just fifty yards away. I was getting full-frame shots of a grizzly for the first time. Again he laid down to cat nap. Like before, he woke up often to check the wind and look around. I remember thinking "what in the world could this grizzly be worried about." For several hours the boar and I moved across the tundra. Resting and grazing in shifts of about an hour each while I photographed his every move from fifty to seventy-five yards away. I had begun to annoy the great boar, he spent more time staring at me. I had crossed that blurred line.

The boar moved even closer to me and drank from the creek then stepped into the water. Laying down in the water on his side, he began to dip his paws into the water and then watch as the water ran off his great claws. Sitting up on his rump he stared at me and yawned. I didn't know the signs. He moved on down the creek grazing a little. Through the viewfinder I watched him bare a big, yellow fang as he growled. Then he suddenly came up the creekbank and charged. I clicked a few pictures and ran out of film. I sat down on the tundra and changed film refusing to look at the beast bearing down on me. When I did look up he was rolling on his back, clearly wishing he was elsewhere as much as I did. The boar rolled over onto his feet and walked away. I did not follow. When I last saw him he was chasing a ground squirrel to its burrow and digging after it. Having more lessons to learn, I didn't let this incident detour my grizzly bear photography.

While hiking an old riverbar overgrown with willow and soapberry bushes I came upon fresh digs, overturned rocks and large piles of soapberries. This was a favorite feeding site for some grizzly. I moved along, slowly watching the bush ahead when I spotted the busy gray grizzly stripping soapberries, leaves and all, from branches. I moved closer and soon the bear caught my scent and walked out of the bush on stiff legs. Out of the brush we moved, the bear paralleling me as I tried to keep distance between us. I knew a mad bear when I saw one and knew enough not to run. I just kept backing up. As we came to the river the bear suddenly laid down, rested his big head on his paws and went to sleep. My desire to photograph the bear overcame my caution and I took a roll of film before backing off a hundred yards. From a distance his sleep seemed real and I returned for more photos. Again I crossed the line.

I sat down just ninety feet from the sleeping bear, and crossed my legs to steady my telephoto lens mounted on a monopod. The bear yawned and stared at me. He rose and with one paw cocked, stared off into the distance. I stood and backed up a few steps. The bear turned and walked toward me, then with powerful swats, he raked both front paws through the air in an aggressive display. He loped for a few steps then at forty feet he charged. Instinctively I threw up my right arm and yelled "Yo!" as loud as I could. The bear skidded to a stop not ten feet away. The wind blew hard but I could easily hear his growling and grinding teeth. Then he turned and walked away, casting mean glances back to make sure I wasn't foolish enough to follow. He returned to his berries.

Later I realized that I had seen and photographed examples of classic displacement behavior. Displacement occurs when two opposite drives engage at the same time. In this case, the grizzly was torn between charging and running away. This indecision of flight or fight was stressful and the bear relieved this tension by sleeping. Another bear might sleep, stare, yawn or even feed to relieve the stress of displacement, but then suddenly charge.

Things had begun to penetrate this thick skull of mine. For several years I carried a dread of grizzlies and left them completely alone. I had been lucky. Several photographers weren't so lucky. Others have been mauled, killed and even eaten by grizzlies they had approached too close for photos. Today approaching grizzlies in Denali National Park is not only dangerous, it is illegal. Interested in stalking grizzlies in the wild for photography? My advice is to take up ballet instead.

Cub Killer

The boar slowly circled the cow and her tiny cub which was cowering under her belly. Like a shark, the boar moved in closer and with each circle he tightened the noose. It was obvious he was after the cub. Suddenly the sow charged but stopped at the last moment just short of the boar who held his ground. She quickly turned back to her cub.

My wife Cindy, our kids Rebecca and Joshua, and I were watching this tense stand off from a high vantage point in Denali National Park. We were on a working vacation to photograph wildlife. We had followed the progress of this blond sow and her unusually small cub for more than ten miles that day. She was on the move. She would run for a while then stop to feed while her cub laid down to rest. We wondered why she would suddenly move to new, unfamiliar country. When the bears reached the braided channels of the east fork of the Toklat River she stopped to feed on soapberries. Cindy spotted the boar moving toward the sow and cub at a fast walk. At first the sow ignored the boar hoping it would move off, but it soon became clear he had something else in mind. After she charged the boar she seemed at a loss what to do next. Her indescision gave the experienced boar the edge. He closed the distance until barely ten feet seperated them. Then the boar charged. The sow counter-charged and the cub ran for its life. The bears exchanged blows but the boar maneuvered past the sow and chased the cub. The sow caught up to the boar and they fought—biting and hurling powerful swats. The boar again broke away and ran after the cub, this time slow enough to follow the scent trail. The boar lost the scent and ran ahead while the sow slowly followed the cub's trail up a hill then back down into willows along the river.

By now the cub was a quarter of a mile ahead of the adults and crossed the east fork and disappeared into tall thick willows where we lost sight of him for good. The sow crossed the river but lost the cub's scent and began to feed. The boar made a wide circle, crossed the river and headed toward the thick willows where we had last seen the cub. The sow fed just 200 yards upstream. The boar was trying to pick up the cub's scent trail and when he too disappeared in the willows we were sure he was close to the cub.

We never saw the outcome of this wilderness drama but we all agreed the cub's chances were slim. It would be a simple matter for the boar to run the cub down and kill it, if he could locate its trail. We blamed the sow's inexperience or lack of aggression or both. As for the boar, he had played this game before—he was a cub killer.

Feeding Grizzlies—Harvesting the Bounty

A grizzly's life is governed by its great appetite. From the time a grizzly leaves the den, after going six or seven months without feeding, it begins to harvest nature's bounties. Sifting scents born by the wind, the bear's powerful olfactory senses bring news of a carcass several miles away, tasty roots, decaying logs containing beetle grubs, or a gopher pocketed within his underground maze.

Mountain grizzlies are omnivorous—vegetarians most of the time and predatory scavengers when the opportunity arises. Different locales obviously have different foods available within the extensive range of the mountain grizzly, and individual bears have particular preferences.

During spring, bears of northern Yellowstone feed mainly on elk carcasses and grass while the grizzlies near Yellowstone Lake make use of grass and spawning cutthroat. Other bears of the high mountains may graze, dig roots, feed on moths and later turn to whitebark pine seeds, pilfered from the caches of red squirrels. No matter where their home range may lie, grizzlies will give the smell of newborn elk calves their immediate attention. Elk calves are not scent-free as some people have suggested, and the calves become a part of the grizzlies' diets whenever possible.

As we have seen, some bears—particularly aggressive males—will kill and eat cubs. Some armchair grizzly researchers suggest that the most important factor determining the range of sows and cubs is isolation from the boars. This idea does not take into account the sows' and cubs' number one priority—access to the best available food sources. I've always found sows with cubs located where the finest food was to be found. These same places were invariably fully stocked with males as well.

A Photo Essay: The Mountain Grizzly

Grizzly sow and cub in the mountainous Alaska interior.

Monarch of the wilderness, a large boar mountain grizzly prowls the river bottoms in the Rocky Mountains along the Athabasca River in Alberta.

Family of grizzly bears loaf among stalks of Alaska boykinia or bear flower—a favorite food.

While digging for biscuit-root in a dry mountain meadow, a Yellowstone grizzly pauses to sniff the air for signs of danger.

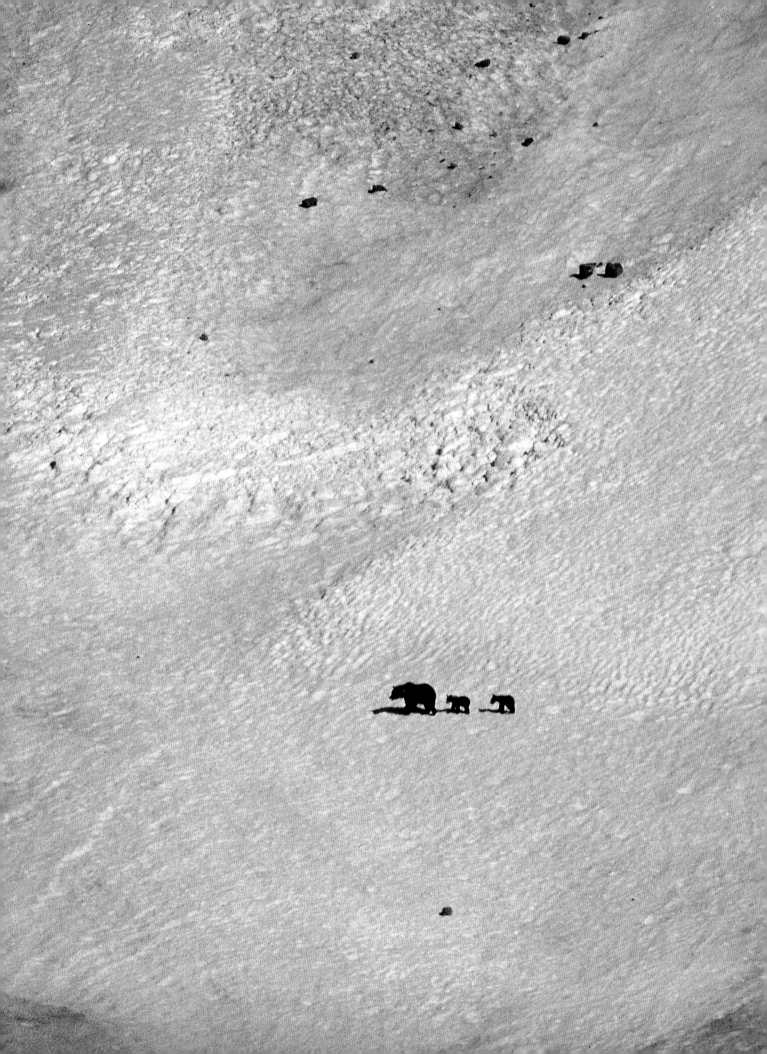

The author photographs grizzlies above timberline. Even with a 1000-mm lens most grizzlies are out of camera range. Minutes after this photo was taken the incoming storm brought lightning strikes all around as we made a hasty retreat from the peak. Grizzlies are not the only danger to a wildlife photographer.

Opposite page:
A mother grizzly leads her twin cubs across a high-altitude snowfield in the mountains of western Wyoming.

A dominant female grizzly bear raises on hind legs as she catches scent of the author. Acute senses of smell and hearing make photography of the shy and dangerous grizzlies difficult.

Sow grizzly and her three cubs slide down a snow drift above timberline.

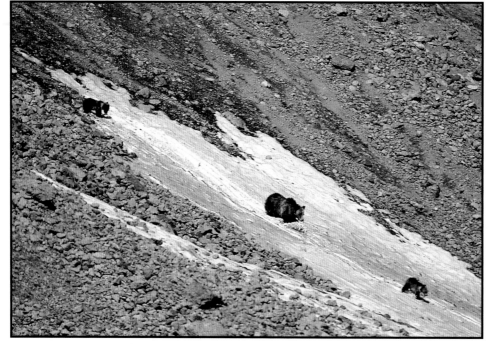

Bears with sore feet from walking and digging on the scree slopes often seek comfort on snowdrifts.

Skid marks left by the grizzly's claws putting on the brakes at the end of a tobaggan ride down a steep snowdrift.

Grizzly bears mothing in typical profile. Moths aestivating during the hot summer months are found deep under the scree.

Following page:
Ever alert, the mother grizzly leads her six-month-old cubs into the peaks far above timberline in search of the army cutworm moths.

Mountain meadows in full bloom are favorite haunts of grizzly bears.

Famous protectors of their cubs, sows can be particulary dangerous. But I found the solitary boars, such as this one bedded in luxurious vegetation, to be more aggressive.

Grizzly sow and cub travel over the tundra of central Alaska.

A yearling cub and its mother sleep on the tundra in Alaska.

Sequence of photos taken at the end of a four-hour session with a large boar grizzly. Finally annoyed by the too-close proximity of the photographer, the bear stares then lays in a creek and threat yawns, classic examples of displacement behavior. The grizzly charges but when I ignored him and changed film he lost his cool and laid down and scratched—another example of displacement.

An angry grizzly suddenly lays down and sleeps. Don't conclude the danger is over because, like this grizzly, a bear will often change its course of action. After standing up on all fours and staring off into the distance, he turns and charges stopping ten feet away only after I yell "Yo" at the top of my lungs.

A big cuddly teddy bear? Don't count on it. A grizzly deciding on flight or fight may seem docile but could suddenly explode.

A grizzly gnaws on an old elk antler.

Like the distant peaks, the tines of an elk antler pierce the Montana sky. Shed during the winter when grizzlies are denned and dormant, the antler will weather and erode and perhaps cause a porcupine, a ground squirrel or even a grizzly bear to pause here. From the forests of Yellowstone National Park to the bush of Alaska's great interior, this wilderness does not belong to the grizzly alone.

Grizzlies come in many sizes and flavors, from dark chocolate to vanilla. This dark cub of the year and its blond mother live in Alaska's Denali National Park.

Inlaid into a lodgepole pine forest and dissected by Pelican Creek, Pelican Valley is the nucleus of grizzly bear habitat in more than 5,000 square miles of greater Yellowstone ecosystem.

Wandering the high, dry meadows of autumn, a silver-tipped subadult grizzly travels extensively within a home range which may be from 36 to 250 square miles. Grizzlies are not territorial and their home ranges overlap. Males generally have larger ranges than females.

Opposite page photo:
A bull elk listens to bugling bulls across a smokey meadow.

Yellowstone cutthroat trout gather in lakes at the mouths of spawning streams each spring attracting not only grizzlies but river otters, eagles, raven, ospreys, white pelicans and black bears.

Mountain goat billy kept his distance, thwarting my attempts to photograph him. That is until three lusty grizzlies appeared heading our way along treacherous ledges. Then, like a lonely mountaineer, he approached me and together we stood and watched the bears skirt the mountain slope below us.

The three grizzlies, sporting new fall coats, bedded down in a patch of ground-hugging, wind-battered subalpine fir at timberline. The sow and yearling cubs would probably den up together for the last time within two months. The yearlings have followed their mother through two summers and are probably weaned.

Headwaters of the Brazeau River divide the backcountry of Jasper and Banff National Parks in western Alberta. This vast sweep of the northern Rocky Mountains is a final refuge for about 100 mountain grizzlies.

Sentry of the mountains, a hoary marmot sits atop a boulder ever alert for its enemies, golden eagles and grizzlies, ready to warn its neighbors with a piercing whistle. Grizzlies excavate tons of earth trying to dig out these tasty treats which often locate their dens under house-sized boulders for obvious reasons.

The spring diet of porcupines is often the same as the mostly vegetarian grizzly. The two are often found feeding in close proximity and for the most part ignore each other.

Spruce woods along the Teklaneeka River give way to a carpet of tundra that skirts the mountains of Alaska's Denali National Park, a wilderness of unparalleled wildlife and beauty.

Alaskan wolf pads through the tundra as it hunts for Arctic ground squirrels.

The grizzlies of Denali wear shaggy, sun-bleached coats during the long Alaskan summer days appearing at a distance like walking straw bales.

Dall sheep inhabit the rugged ridges and flanks of the Alaska Mountain Range. A ewe nuzzles her lamb and keeps a sharp eye for the sight of bears and wolves who prey on the sheep. Sighting danger the sheep sprint for the safety of cliffs.

These photos were taken only minutes apart and show the physical differences between black and grizzly bears. The black bear feeding on fresh sprouts of grass was clearly nervous, watching his backtrail and testing the wind for signs of danger. The grizzly paused to smell the fresh scent of the nearby black bear and suddenly switched from grazer to predator. Moving uphill, the grizzly began to parallel the blackie's course stalking by sight. When the grizzly reached a position 100 feet from the black bear he charged, crashing through the brush. The startled blackie was going full throttle in two jumps and managed to stay ahead of the grizzly. I could keep track of their progress by the commotion made by the bruins poking holes through the scenery. The chase broke off as the black bear shimmied up a tall, skinny lodgepole pine.

Peaks along the Continental Divide split waters into the seperate drainages of Montana's Madison River and Idaho's Henrys Fork of the Snake River. Important grizzly habitat in the Yellowstone ecosystem is being lost due to vacation home sprawl and deforestation.

Symbolic of grizzly country everywhere, habitat loss is escalating leaving the future of grizzly bears blurred.

Nesting great gray owls and goshawks attest to the diversity of this wildlife community under seige.

Cooling off during the heat of courtship a pair of Canadian mountain grizzlies pause to bathe in a mountain stream. The female holds her head low in submission of her much larger and more powerful mate. Mating takes place during the spring in late May and into June. Females often are eight or nine years old before they have their first cubs.

Love-sick males are often playful and gentle but persistent, staying with one female for a week or more.

Mating may last for twenty minutes or more with the male grasping the sides of the female with his powerful front legs and claws. Talk about holding power.

Sow grizzly leads her string of triplets up a snow-drift. These cubs are about five months old and will stay with their mother for about two more years. Cubs weigh between five and ten pounds when they leave the den in early spring.

Grizzly cubs are born in their mothers' winter den during January or February. This den in Yellowstone was dug under a large tree on a steep hillside. This is a view from inside the den looking out.

A six-month-old Alaska grizzly already exhibits the dished profile and massive jaw characteristic of their species.

Though twins are the rule, single cubs are common; however, they must spend hours entertaining themselves.

These yearling cubs and their mother are busy picking Alaskan blueberries. They are more than a year and a half old and will spend the coming winter with their mother denning as a family unit.

There are always enough blueberries to go around, and many wildlife species relish them including this red-backed vole.

A sow grizzly leads her three yearlings over a mountain pass. Learning to be grizzlies by her example, the yearlings will soon be on their own. Their survival will depend on how well they learned.

A stand off between a sow and her cub and a boar in Denali National Park. The sow and her small cub had been on the move all day. Eventually the boar came into sight, explaining the sow's restless behavior. The boar and sow (the light-colored bear in picture below) charged and counter-charged, and the cub ran for its life. The photographer never saw the outcome of the drama, but the cub's chances of getting way unscathed were not good.

Opposite page:
Nose to nose, grizzlies square off for battle. On their own for the first time in a dangerous world, the sibling subadults find security together and cling to each other, for the time being. They feed, sleep and engage in mock battle together. Such play tends to get rough but encourages self confidence and aggression which all grizzlies need to survive. Subadults slowly range into new country and begin to develop a home range of their own.

Cubs learn to feed by following the example of their mothers. This cub takes a bite of boykinia or bear flower leaf. The pink flowers belong to dwarf fireweed.

This grizzly family is grazing on soap berries.

A large boar grizzly grazes on succulent grass. Grass makes up 50 percent of the diet of many mountain grizzlies.

Grizzlies are opportunists. Always ready to switch from vegetarian to predator, the mountain grizzly is equipped to handle anything from mice to moose. An Alberta grizzly in Jasper National Park feeds on a moose for over a week, burying it with dirt and gravel and chasing coyotes and ravens away. Another Jasper grizzly takes time out from grazing on grass to catch a vole. The bear pounced on the vole just like a pouncing fox or coyote.

A grizzly sow in Alaska's Denali National Park and Preserve digs for Arctic ground squirrels while her cubs practice their techniques. When the sow captured a ground squirrel she quickly ate it without sharing. One cub tries to force its way to the tasty morsel. The sow tenderizes the squirrel with bone-smashing crunches before swallowing.

A ground squirrel harvests seeds from a tall grass stalk. These rodents are on every predator's menu and are ever alert, ready to escape down subterranean burrows. Their shallow burrows are no protection from a grizzly's powerful digging equipment.

Grizzlies interrupt intense feeding sessions with numerous cat naps, usually under some cover.

A grizzly bear's nose is key to its survival. These intelligent animals possess a detailed memory of where and when to find food. Periodic forays through their home range to check on food sources assures they will be around as foods become available. Raging rivers and mountain ranges are no barriers to these scouting trips.

A grizzly's fondness for the roots of hedysarum, or wild sweet pea, often leaves acres of ground torn up by the bear's digging.

A grizzly feeding on fresh shoots of equizitum (horsetail) moves slowly through a patch snipping off the tops of the plant. Horsetails are a favorite spring mainstay.

A grizzly foraging on a high mountain ridge in Yellowstone attracts the attention of a pair of ravens. Always on the lookout for a meal, ravens make their living by poking their big, black bills into their neighbors' business.

Each fall grizzlies must put on enough weight to last the upcoming six-month fast in their winter dens. This subadult grizzly forces a rock from its bed to lick up ants and beetles. Nothing is too small to be overlooked during the fall feeding frenzy. Powerful arms open up the tough, dry earth to reveal roots of the biscuit-root then lift a small root to its mouth.

Far above timberline a mountain grizzly tips a rock to check for moths underneath. Mothing bears use the pads on the bottoms of their front feet, not their claws, to flip rocks. Few bear foods offer so much pure protein for the effort than the moths.

The moths migrate to the mountain peaks to aestivate in aggregations under the scree. As many as a dozen grizzlies fed at one time. Clark's nutcrackers by the hundreds join the grizzlies to feed on the moths. We watched the nutcrackers catching moths under rocks on the edges of cliffs. Ravens and black bears also fed on the moths.

The moth eaters were more often than not sows with cubs. These families may have trouble getting enough nutrition from other food sources. Even though huckleberries hung heavy on the slopes below timberline, these grizzly families spent the majority of their time foraging on the moths.

A sow grizzly and her yearling cub graze on grass and then settle down for nursing.

A large dominant sow grizzly leads her twins down a gravel road in Denali National Park. Here bears have the right of way.

A subadult grizzly habituated to humans walks past a boat near a lakeside resort. Learning to associate people with food, as this young bear is doing, results in a very dangerous situation for bears and people.

When in bear country hang food. At camps above timberline we hung our food away from bears. The grizzlies gave us no trouble but once a pack rat gnawed our tether and the food dropped more than 700 feet down a cliff, pulverizing the contents—a new recipe for trail mix.

Cooking in bear country requires a clean camp and low-scent meals to protect both man and bears.

Visitors crowding two grizzlies in Yellowstone Park are herded back to the road by a park ranger.

A grizzly wearing a collar growls at his enemy—man. This bear frequented a popular hiking area in Glacier National Park in northern Montana and was responsible for mauling two hikers.

The tracks of a grizzly are a powerful reminder of just who rules the wilderness. Man is the trespasser.

Hikers encounter a grizzly in Montana's Glacier National Park. Are our wilderness national parks wildlife preserves or recreational playgrounds?

A wild, free-roaming mountain grizzly travels through elk calving grounds in northern Yellowstone National Park. The bear leaves an endless line of tracks across mountains and forests, the domain of the grizzly—monarch of the mountains.

References

Craighead, Frank C., Jr. *Track of the Grizzly*. San Francisco, California: Sierra Club Books, 1979.

Herrero, Stephen. *Bear Attacks: Their Causes and Avoidance*. New York, New York: Lyons and Burford, 1985.

Russell, Andy. *Grizzly Country*. Alfred A. Knopf, Inc., 1967.

Schullery, Paul. *The Bears of Yellowstone*. Yellowstone National Park, Wyoming: Yellowstone Library and Museum Association, 1980.

Seton, Ernest Thompson. *The Biography of a Grizzly*. Originally published: New York: Century, 1900.

Wright, William H. *The Grizzly Bear*. New York: Scribner, 1909.

Also by Michael Quinton
ISBN 0-88839-423-3

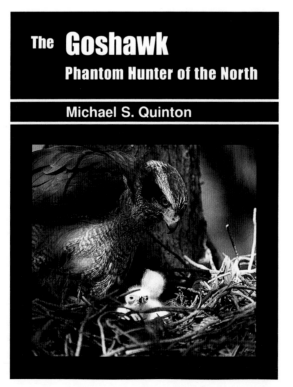

The **Goshawk**
Phantom Hunter of the North

Michael S. Quinton